I
don't like
it!

For Klaus and Audrey

Copyright ©1989 by Ruth Brown.
This paperback edition first published in 2001 by Andersen Press Ltd. The rights of Ruth Brown to be identified as the author and illustrator of this work have been asserted by her in accordance with the Copyright, Designs and Patents Act, 1988.
First published in Great Britain in 1989 by Andersen Press Ltd., 20 Vauxhall Bridge Road, London SW1V 2SA.
Published in Australia by Random House Australia Pty., 20 Alfred Street, Milsons Point, Sydney, NSW 2061.
All rights reserved. Colour separated in Switzerland by Photolitho AG, Zurich.
Printed and bound in China.

10 9 8 7 6 5 4 3 2 1

British Library Cataloguing in Publication Data available.

ISBN 0 86264 230 2

This book has been printed on acid-free paper

With grateful thanks to Anne Wilkinson, designer of the doll

I don't like it!

Ruth Brown

Andersen Press · London

The little doll sighed – "I'm sad!" she cried.
"I knew things would change. I don't like it!
It's not the same since that puppy came
And it's such a shame. I don't like it!

"She loves him more than me, I'm sure
They play all the time and I hate it!
But if I want to play, then they just go away –
So why shouldn't I say: I don't like it!

"Perhaps it's just me. Hey, toys! Can you see
How everything's changed. Do you like it?"
Ted lay on his bed and raising his head
He sleepily said: "I don't mind it!

"It means I can rest which is what I do best
'Cos I'm lazy and fat and I like it.
I snooze and I dream that I'm eating ice-cream
With the honey-bee queen. Yes! I love it!"

"I might have known you wouldn't moan.
I'll ask Jack-in-the-Box if he likes it.
Hey, you over there! I've just asked the bear
If he thinks it's fair. Do you mind it?"

"Odd as it seems, it is one of my dreams
To be quiet and still and I love it.
My head aches so when I have to go
Jumping to and fro. I can't stand it!

"And when I'm boxed up tight, in the dark dark night,
I quake and I shake and I hate it!
But when I'm out and I'm lying about
There's no shadow of a doubt – that I like it!"

"Well the mice aren't like you – they want something to do!
I'll call them and see if they mind it."
So she knelt on the floor to knock on their door
And asked like before: "Do you like it?"

A tiny grey mouse stepped out of the house
And said: "Yes, we really enjoy it!
We've never had time to clean up the grime
And to polish and shine — and we love it!"

"Listen to you! You're too good to be true!
If they'd got a cat, would you like it?"
But the mouse turned around and with hardly a sound
Started sweeping the ground. She did like it!

"I'm the only one who wants any fun!"
The little doll sighed — but she wasn't —

For when later on everybody had gone
And the house was totally silent…

Someone else came that way, also wanting to play
Saw the doll where it lay — and he liked it!

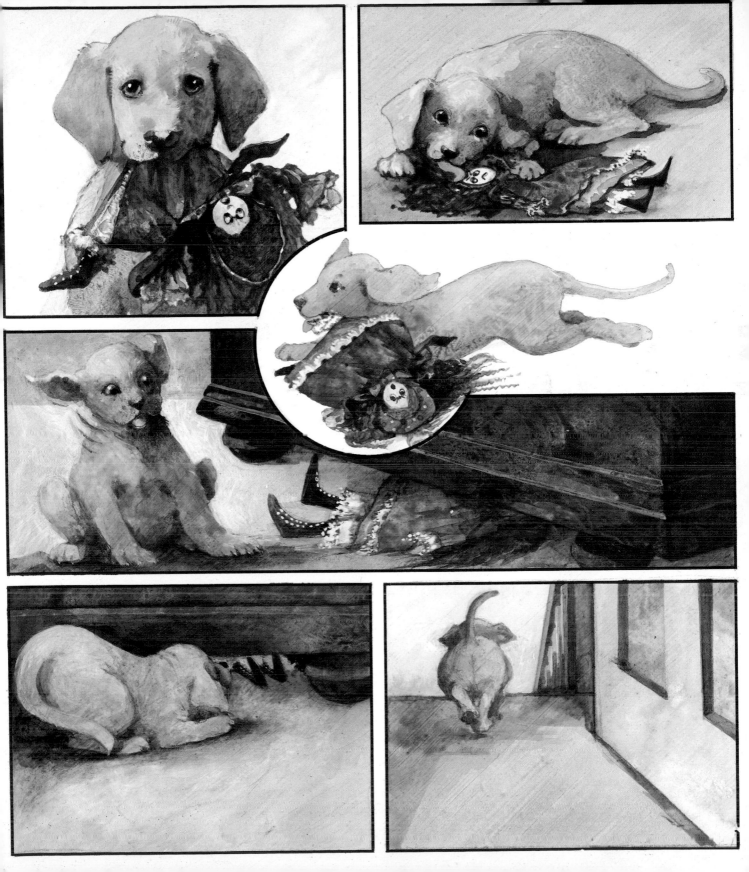

That night Mum said: "It's time for bed.
Where's your doll gone? Can you see it?"
So they searched everywhere – on the floor, on the stair –
But it just wasn't there! "We can't find it!

"It's lost, you see – where can it be?"
The little girl sobbed. "I want it!"
"Don't cry so, dear – it must be near.
Look! Puppy's here! Go fetch it!

"He's done it too! It's as if he knew
That your doll was there – and he found it!
Well, I'll say goodnight and switch off the light.
Will you be all right, now you've got it?"

But there came no reply, not a stir, not a sigh,
For the girl was asleep now she'd found it.
And the little doll smiled, snuggled close to the child,
With a cry soft and mild: "That's more like it!"